The

SHOUT!

THE VOICE OF VICTORY FOR KIDS

Joke Book

heirborne

The *Shout!* Joke Book
ISBN 1-57562-238-6
30-1225

09 08 07 06 05 04 03 02 01 00   10 9 8 7 6 5 4 3 2 1

ripture is from *The Holy Bible, New King James Version,*
ght © 1982 by Thomas Nelson, Inc.

Heirborne

eland Ministries
xas 76192-0001

r: Jokes marked "Anonymous" are jokes sent in by
e of Victory for Kids readers who did not include
ditor

Contents

Dear Reader,

We had no idea when we began "The Joke Spot" on the back of Shout! in 1996 that it would soon become one of our readers' favorite features. Since then, every month we've received letter after letter punctuated with a joke.

Why? We believe it's because kids, better than anyone else, understand that strength comes through joy. After all, the Bible says in Proverbs 17:22, "A merry heart does good, like medicine."

May this fun-filled book packed with jokes from kids all over the world be a continual testimony of the joy the Lord gives. God has given laughter to His children...so go ahead and have some fun!

The Shout! The Voice of Victory
for Kids Staff (Hee-hee!)

Bible Jokes

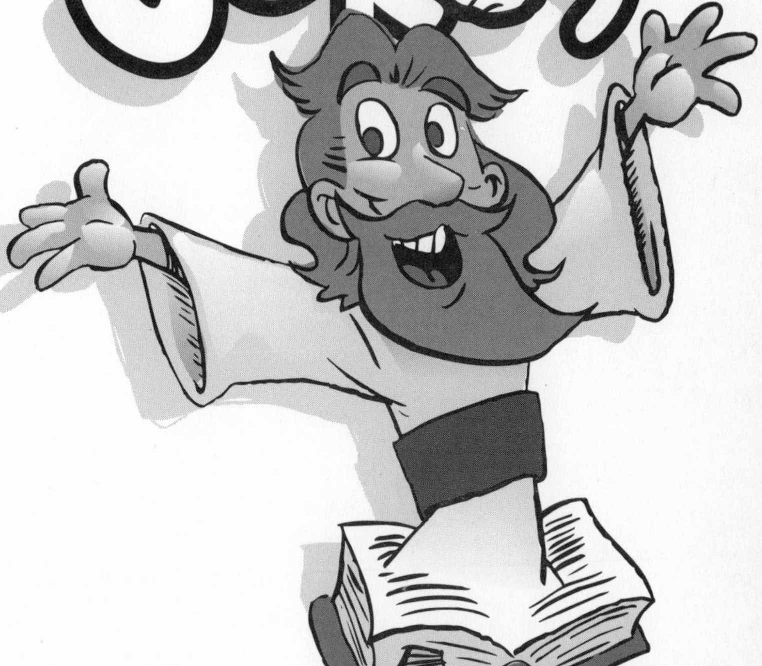

Q: Where is tennis mentioned in the Bible?
A: When Joseph served in Pharaoh's court!
Savanna, age 11
Arizona

Q: Who was the first hot-rod racer
recorded in the Bible?
A: Aaron, because he dragged his rod
across the desert!
Lukas, age 8
Canada

Q: What did Jesus and the whale that
swallowed Jonah have in common?
A: Jesus had dinner with a sinner,
and the whale had a sinner for dinner!
Rachel, age 12
Canada

Q: What kind of light did Noah use on the ark?

A: A floodlight!

Elise, age 12
Michigan

Q: Why didn't they play cards on Noah's ark?

A: Because Noah sat on the deck!

Christina
Minnesota

Q: Was there any money on Noah's ark?

A: Yes, the duck had a bill, the frog had a greenback and the skunk had a scent!

Savanna, age 11
Arizona

Q: What was Noah's wife's name?

A: She had Noah name!

Andrew, age 8
Canada

Q: What kind of animal skin did Adam and Eve wear in the garden?

A: Bare skin!

Misti
Texas

Q: What day of the week did Noah
   march the animals into the ark?
A: Twos-day!

> Omar, age 12
> Florida

Q: How can you tell David was older
   than Goliath?
A: Because David rocked Goliath to sleep!

> Savanna, age 11
> Arizona

Q: What did Jonah feel like when he
   was swallowed by the whale?
A: A little down in the mouth!

> Gabriel, age 9
> Arizona

Q: Who was the first submarine captain
   under the sea?
A: Jonah!

> Ima, age 8
> New Guinea

Q: Who was the greatest speaker in the Bible?
A: Samson, because he brought the
   house down!

> Jennifer, age 11
> California

Q: When was the first baseball game recorded in the Bible?

A: In the beginning (big inning)!

Lukas, age 8
Canada

Q: Where did the rooster crow when all the world could hear him?

A: In Noah's ark!

Johanna, age 13

Q: Why do they always have the Bible in court?

A: Because one of the books is Judges!

Mallory, age 5
Florida

Q: In what season did Eve eat the
forbidden fruit?
A: Early in the Fall!

Rachel, age 11
Michigan

Q: What book in the Bible is a mineral?
A: Micah!

Nason
Texas

Q: What sport was popular in the
Old Testament?
A: Baseball, because Adam stole second
and he and Eve were put out.
Cain made a hit and Noah put the
dove out on a fly.
Abraham made a sacrifice, King
Solomon bought a diamond and
Ruth wanted to get home!

Natalie, age 12
Indiana

Q: What man in the Bible had no parents?
A: Joshua, the son of Nun!

Kristin
Texas

Q: What did Noah use to see out of
the ark's window?
A: Windshield vipers!
> Janelle, age 13
> Louisiana

Q: Why was Abraham so wise?
A: Because he knew a Lot!
> Amanda, age 12

Q: Who was the straightest man in the Bible?
A: Joseph, because Pharaoh made him a ruler!
> Brad, age 10
> Arizona

Q: What time of day was Adam born?
A: A little before Eve!
> Savanna, age 11
> Arizona

Q: Why couldn't Cain please God
   with his offering?
A: Because he just wasn't Abel!
                    Seth, age 9
                    Colorado

Q: How do we know Adam was a fast runner?
A: He was the first in the human race!
                    Janelle, age 13
                    Louisiana

Q: When was money first mentioned in
   the Bible?
A: When the dove brought the greenback to the ark!
                    Savanna, age 11
                    Arizona

Q: Why wasn't much fruit allowed in
   the ark?
A: Because only pairs were allowed!
                    Denise
                    Texas

Q: What animal took the most baggage
into the ark?

A: The elephant. He took his trunk
while the fox and rooster only
took a brush and comb!

> Savanna, age 11
> Arizona

Q: Why did Elijah go to heaven in a
fiery chariot?

A: Because he was on fire for the Lord!

> Peter, age 11
> Pennsylvania

Q: How was Moses able to part the
Red Sea?

A: He used a sea-saw!

> Jonathan, age 9
> Kentucky

Q: Why did Joseph's brothers toss him
in a pit?

A: They must have thought it was a
good opening for a young man!

> Natalie, age 12
> Indiana

Q: Who was the biggest sinner in the Bible?
A: Moses, because he broke all 10 commandments at once!
> Jennifer, age 11
> California

Q: Where was King Solomon's temple?
A: On the side of his head!
> Cole, age 8
> Canada

Q: Who was the most successful physician in the Bible?
A: Job, because he had the most patience (patients)!
> Savanna, age 11
> Arizona

Animal Jokes

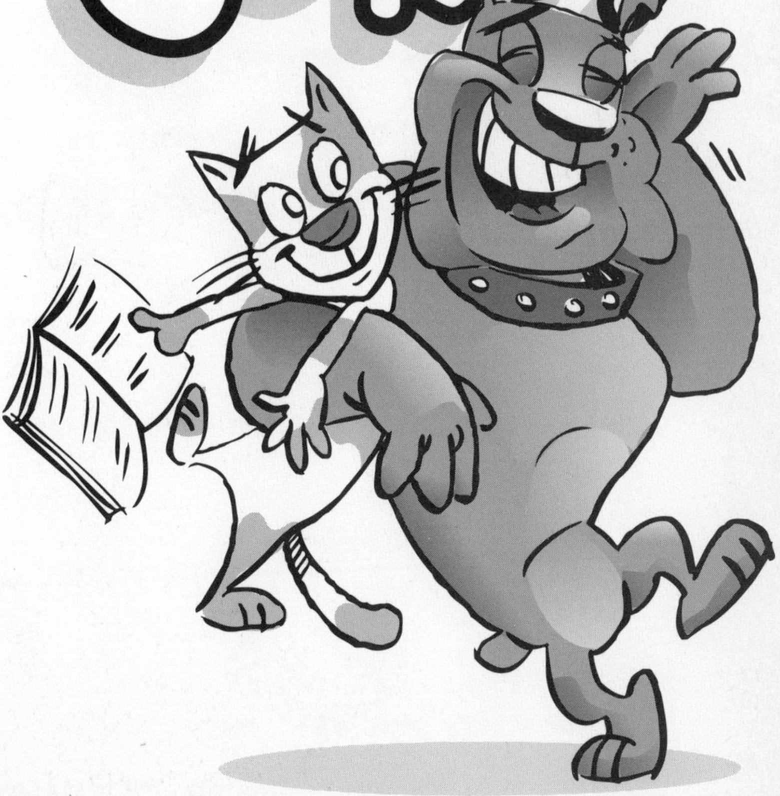

Q: What do snakes learn in school?
A: Hiss-s-s-story!
                    Timothy, age 8

Q: What did the judge say when a
   skunk walked in?
A: "Odor in the court!"
                    Ryan, age 11
                    Canada

Q: How do you keep a skunk from smelling?
A: Just hold its nose!
                    Mandy
                    Canada

Q: Why do some cows wear bells?
A: Because their horns don't work!
                    Patrick
                    Alabama

Q: What do you get when you cross an
   owl with an oyster?
A: An animal that drops pearls of wisdom!
                Janelle
                Arkansas

Q: What dog keeps the best time?
A: A watchdog!
                Dan
                Ohio

Q: What games do baby boars play with
   their parents?
A: Pig-a-boo!
                Jarrod, age 10
                Texas

Q: What do you get from an invisible cow?
A: Evaporated milk!
                Jennifer, age 12
                Missouri

Q: What is green and has 16 wheels?
A: An alligator on roller skates!
                Zeanne, age 12
                New York

Q: What did the canary say when his bird cage fell apart?
A: "Cheap, cheap!"

Calie
Wisconsin

Q: What's black, white and red all over?
A: A zebra with a sunburn!

T.J., age 13
Georgia

Q: How can you tell a pig is a superstar?
A: He's the one in the dark glasses!

Nicci, age 12
Ohio

Q: Where does a 1,000-pound monkey sit?
A: Anywhere he wants!

Amber
Missouri

Q: What does a 200-pound mouse say?
A: "Here, kitty, kitty!"

Joshua, age 11
California

Q: Why did the cats get married?
A: They were a purr-fect match!

Mikia
Florida

Q: What did the young porcupine say
when it bumped into the cactus?
A: "Is that you, Mom?!"

Grant, age 9
Texas

Q: What do you call a cow that eats grass?
A: A lawn moo-er!

Stephanie
Canada

Q: How do rabbits keep themselves looking good?
A: They use hare spray!

Angelique, age 7
Iowa

Q: What do you call a horse that plays a guitar?
A: A rockin' horse!

> Steven, age 4
> Texas

Q: How do cows get where they want to go?
A: In auto-moo-biles!

> Jared, age 11
> California

Q: Why did the pig keep driving around the parking lot?
A: Because he couldn't find a porking place!

> Sarah
> Texas

Q: Why do bulldogs have flat faces?
A: Because they keep running into parked cars!

Zac
Australia

Q: Why did the dog cross the road?
A: It wanted to get to the barking lot!

Corey, age 10
Oklahoma

Q: Why do birds fly south for the winter?
A: Because it's too far to walk!

Sarah, age 9
Australia

Q: What is the easiest way to catch a fish?
A: Have someone throw it to you!

Anna, age 9
Kentucky

Q: What did the preaching horse say?
A: "Let your naaaay be naaaay and let your yeaaaa be yeaaaa!"

Simona
Texas

Q: What's black, white, white, black, black, white and green?

A: Three skunks fighting over a pickle!

Rebecca, age 7
Texas

Q: What is a kangaroo's favorite year?

A: Leap year!

Amanda, age 10
Virginia

Q: What is a flea's favorite shopping place?

A: The flea market!

Adine, age 9
New Jersey

Q: What do you call mail sent to a cat?

A: Kitty letter!

Ryan, age 11
Canada

Q: What kind of bird is at every meal?
A: A swallow!

> Mandy, age 11
> Canada

Q: Why does a hummingbird hum?
A: Because he doesn't know the words!

> Kendra
> Ohio

Q: Why did the turkey join a band?
A: Because he had drumsticks!

> Jacob, age 10
> New York

Q: Why couldn't the pony talk?
A: He was a little horse!

> Johanna, age 13

Q: Where do you find a turtle with no legs?
A: Right where you left him!

> Andrew, age 8
> Canada

Q: What is a good way to keep a dog off the street?
A: Put him in the barking lot!

Stephen
Canada

Q: Which is the biggest ant?
A: The gi<u>ant</u>!

Q: Which is the second biggest ant?
A: The eleph<u>ant</u>!

Q: Which is the bossiest ant?
A: The tyr<u>ant</u>!

Q: Which is the dumbest ant?
A: The ignor<u>ant</u>!

Q: Which ant lives in a house?
A: The occup<u>ant</u>!

Q: Which ant is in the army?
A: The serge<u>ant</u>!

Sarah
Texas

Q: What do you call a cow that hates to be milked?
A: A milk dud!

Melissa, age 12
Oklahoma

Q: Why was the pig mad at the hog?
A: The hog squealed on him!

Michael, age 8
North Carolina

Q: What do frogs eat for lunch?
A: Flyburgers!

Caroline, age 8
Illinois

Q: Why did the bubble gum cross the road?
A: Because it was stuck to the chicken's foot!

Emily, age 9
Michigan

Q: Why did the duck go to college?
A: Because he wanted to be a wise-quacker!

Hannah
Iowa

Q: What did the duck say when she bought some lipstick?
A: "Put it on my bill!"
David, age 9
Minnesota

Q: Why did the cactus cross the road?
A: It was stuck to the chicken's back!
Diana, age 11
Alabama

Q: What goes "tick-tock, woof-woof"?
A: A watchdog!
Jennie, age 9
Canada

Q: What kind of insect does well in school?
A: A spelling bee!
Charles, age 13
Texas

Q: How do you catch a unique bird?
A: U-nique up on it!

Q: How do you catch a tame bird?
A: You do it the tame way!
                    Danielle, age 8
                    Canada

Q: What did one duck say to the other duck?
A: "Duck! There's a bridge!"
                    Justin
                    Canada

Q: What do geese do in a traffic jam?
A: They honk a lot!
                    Crystal, age 11
                    Tennessee

Q: How does the farmer move his cows?
A: In a moo-ving van!
                    Elisha, age 8

Q: What do you get when you cross a cocker
   spaniel, a poodle and a rooster?
A: A cocker-poodle-doo!
                    Tempestt, age 9
                    Australia

Q: What is big, gray and wears glass
   slippers?
A: Cinderelephant!

> Laurel, age 8
> Canada

Q: Where do sheep like to go on vacation?
A: To the Baa-haa-maas!

> Kristin, age 10
> Montana

Q: How does a bull buy his food?
A: He charges it!

> Sarah, age 10
> Florida

Q: What's the cheapest pet to feed?
A: A giraffe, because when you feed it,
   a little goes a long way!

> Joey, age 9
> Nebraska

Q: What airplane do dogs fly on?
A: Flea-W-A!

> Kristen, age 9
> Texas

Q: What goes "zzub, zzub, zzub"?
A: A bee flying backward!
Danette, age 10
Arkansas

Q: What has two heads, one tail, four legs on one side, and two legs on the other?
A: A horse with a lady riding sideways!
Sarah, age 8
Arkansas

Q: How can you tell an elephant likes to travel?
A: He always has his trunk with him!
Jeremy, age 10
California

Q: What is gray, has large ears and goes "squeak, squeak"?
A: An elephant wearing new shoes!
Kristen, age 8
Texas

Q: What do you call a cow with no legs?
A: Ground beef!

Melissa, age 12
Oklahoma

Q: How did the turtle get across the road so fast?
A: He rode on the chicken's back!

Timmy, age 8

Q: What happens when a cat eats a lemon?
A: It turns into a sourpuss!

Jennifer, age 12
West Virginia

Q: How do chickens save money when they go shopping?
A: They use their coop-ons!

Desirae, age 9

Q: Where do sheep get their hair cut?
A: At the baa-baa shop!
> Anne, age 6
> Canada

Q: What do you get when you cross a
   cow and axes?
A: Milk and hackers!
> Erica, age 10
> Texas

Q: Why did the mouse eat his cheese?
A: Because he was hungry!
> Dusti, age 10
> Mississippi

Q: Why did the man run over the cow?
A: Because he wanted fresh meat and milk!
> Emily, age 9
> Mississippi

Q: What do you get when you cross
   potatoes with an elephant?
A: Mashed potatoes!
> Timothy, age 8
> Mississippi

Q: Why are elephants always ready to
   go swimming?
A: Because they always have their
   trunks with them!
                    Joey, age 9
                    Nebraska

Q: What does an eagle like to write with?
A: A bald-point pen!
                    David, age 10
                    Illinois

Q: How do turtles give cash?
A: They shell it out!
                    Michael, age 8
                    North Carolina

Q: What keys are too big to carry in
   your pocket?
A: Donkeys, turkeys and monkeys!
                    Chelsea, age 9
                    Canada

Q: How did the bulldog get a burned nose?
A: He tried to iron the wrinkles out of his face!

Justin, age 11
Canada

Q: What did the cow say at night?
A: "The mooon is very pretty!"

Simona
Texas

Q: How did the cowboy count his cows?
A: He used a cow-culator!

Donald
Nevada

Q: Why do fish live in salt water?
A: Because pepper makes them sneeze!

Amber, age 9
Oklahoma

Q: What do you get when you cross a pig, a sheep and a fir tree?
A: A pork-ewe-pine!

Jarrod, age 10
Texas

Animal Jokes **31**

Q: Why did the cats have kittens?
A: Because they wanted a purr-fect, complete family!

Deanna, age 7
Ohio

Q: Why did the farmer feed his cow money?
A: He wanted rich milk!

Jennifer, age 12
Missouri

Q: What do you get when you cross a caterpillar and a bigmouth?
A: A walkie-talkie!

Jessica, age 11
Tennessee

Q: What did the bat say to the other bat?
A: "Do you want to hang around?"

Elisha
Michigan

Q: What do you call a sleeping bull?
A: A bull-dozer!

Samuel, age 10
Texas

Q: What do you get when you cross a
   toad and a stool?
A: A toadstool!

> Theron, age 13
> Texas

Q: Why do cows have horns?
A: Because they're moo-sical!

> Patrick
> Alabama

Q: Why didn't the chicken cross the road?
A: Because he was a chicken!

> Sara, age 8
> Georgia

Q: What do bears eat?
A: Bear-ies!

> Deidre, age 9
> West Virginia

Q: What do you get when you cross a
   cow and a porcupine?
A: A steak with a built-in toothpick!

> Joey, age 9
> Nebraska

Q: How can you talk to a pig?
A: Use pig latin!

Nicci, age 12
Ohio

Q: What do you get when you cross a
   zebra and a horse?
A: A horse in jail!

Arista, age 8
Kentucky

Q: What do rabbits fly?
A: A hare-plane!

Kristen, age 9
Texas

Q: Why do chickens lay their eggs?
A: Because if they drop them, they will break!

Felicitee
Washington

Q: Where do fish keep their money?
A: In riverbanks!

Christine, age 9
Arizona

Q: Why did the owl say, "Tweet, tweet"?
A: He didn't give a hoot!

> Jessica, age 10
> Kentucky

Q: Which season do kangaroos like best?
A: Springtime!

> Jordan, age 11
> California

Q: What do cows wear in Hawaii?
A: Moo-moos!

> Lotoya, age 9
> Louisiana

Q: Where does the bull get his messages?
A: From the bull-etin board!

> Tessa, age 12
> South Dakota

Q: What is the greatest song in bee history?
A: "Stinging in the rain!"

> Lee, age 7
> Texas

Q: What do you call a nervous cow?
A: A milkshake!

> Melissa, age 12
> Oklahoma

Q: Why did the turkey cross the road?
A: To prove he wasn't a chicken!

> Tempestt, age 9
> Australia

Q: How do you catch a squirrel?
A: Climb up a tree and act like a nut!

> Nicholas, age 9
> New York

Q: What do flies do all day?
A: Fly around!

> Justin
> Canada

Q: Which day of the week does a fish hate the most?
A: Fry-day!

> Jenny
> Florida

Q: What kind of fish is greedy?
A: A sel-fish!

Cassidy
California

Q: What do you see in a chicken coop?
A: Hen-tertainment!

Sarah, age 7
Canada

Q: What kind of key won't open a door?
A: A monkey!

Sarah, age 10
Florida

Q: What has a trunk, two gray ears and a tail?
A: A mouse on vacation!

Anonymous

Q: What kind of dictionary do spiders use?
A: Web-ster's Dictionary!

Nason
Texas

Q: What did the sparrow say to his girlfriend?
A: "You're real tweet!"
        Jessica, age 11

Q: Why do elephants' tusks stick out?
A: Their parents couldn't afford braces!
        Jared, age 13
        California

Q: Where do cows go on vacation?
A: Cow-lifornia!
        Jared, age 11
        California

Q: What time is it when an elephant sits on your fence?
A: Time to get a new fence!
        Anonymous

Q: Where do you get cocoa from?
A: A brown cow!

Ronisha, age 11
Georgia

Q: Why was Miss Cow upset?
A: Her boyfriend was in a bullfight!

Crystal, age 11
Tennessee

Q: When a pig burns himself, what does he put on it?
A: Oink-ment!

Corrie, age 8
Canada

Q: Why do skunks smell?
A: Because they have noses!

Lauren, age 9
California

Q: What's tan, brown, tan, brown, green, tan and brown?
A: Three lions fighting over a pickle!

Erica, age 10
Texas

Q: What did the snail say when it rode on the turtle's back?

A: "Whee!"

J.D., age 10
Pennsylvania

Q: What do you call a melted, chocolate-covered rabbit?

A: A runny bunny!

R.J., age 8
Florida

Q: Why was the cow afraid?

A: Because she was a cow-ard!

Brad, age 10
Arizona

Q: What is a duck's favorite snack?

A: Cheese and quackers!

Nicholas, age 9
New York

Q: Why are elephants so wrinkly?
A: Have you ever tried to iron one?!
> Kristine, age 10
> Canada

Q: Where does a frog hang its coat?
A: In the croak-room!
> Joanna, age 10
> England

Q: Where do tough chickens come from?
A: From hard-boiled eggs!
> Christine, age 9
> Arizona

Q: Why do four-legged animals make bad dancers?
A: They have two left feet!
> Donald
> Nevada

Q: Why did the duck cross the road?
A: Because the chicken was on vacation!
> Amber, age 8
> Texas

Q: What do frogs drink?
A: Croak-a-cola!

> Nathan
> Wisconsin

Q: Why did the dog jump in the lake?
A: To catch a catfish!

> Laketha, age 8
> New York

Q: When did the bedbugs get married?
A: In the spring!

> Maria, age 8
> New York

Q: What is green, black and white all over?
A: A turtle that thinks it's a zebra!

> Brittany, age 9
> Virginia

Q: What kind of car does a cat drive?
A: A cat-illac!

> Kristen, age 9
> Texas

Q: What do you call two cats?
A: A purr!

Mattie, age 8
Texas

Q: What did the Spanish farmer say to his chicken?
A: "Oh lay!"

Tempestt, age 9
Australia

Q: Why did the dog wag its tail?
A: Because no one would wag it for him!

Adrienne, age 9
Texas

Q: Why didn't the pony win the race?
A: He was horsing around!

Jennifer, age 12
Missouri

Q: What is it called when a duck scores
in basketball?
A: A slam-duck!

Christina
Minnesota

Q: What do you get when you cross a
hen and a shark?
A: A chicken of the sea!

Callan
Canada

Q: What animal has the head of a cat,
the tail of a cat, purrs like a cat
and acts like a cat, but isn't a cat?
A: A kitten!

Danielle, age 13
Michigan

Q: What do cows like to read?
A: The moos-paper!

Cara, age 12
Oklahoma

Q: Where do cows go on vacation?
A: Moo York!

Donald
Nevada

Q: What's gray and goes around and
around and around?
A: An elephant stuck in a
revolving door!

Eve, age 12
West Virginia

Q: What's as big as an elephant but
weighs nothing at all?
A: An elephant's shadow!

Melissa
Oklahoma

Q: What hurts more than a giraffe
with a sore throat?
A: A centipede with sore feet!

Sara, age 8
Georgia

Q: What do you do when you catch
your dog eating a dictionary?
A: You take the words right out of
his mouth!

Justin

Q: What do you call an elephant falling
out of bed?
A: An earthwake!

Jeff, age 11
Texas

Q: What do cats read?
A: A catalog!

Michael, age 6
England

Q: What do you call a deer with no eyes?
A: No eye-dear (idea)!

Anonymous

Q: What do you call a dog with no legs?
A: It doesn't matter—he won't
come anyway!

Robby, age 8
Pennsylvania

Q: Why is it hard to talk with a goat around?
A: Because he always butts in!
Olivia

Q: What is black, white and red?
A: A zebra with the flu!
Ronisha, age 11
Georgia

Q: What do pigs write with?
A: Pig-pens!
Nicci, age 12
Ohio

Q: What did the skunk say to the man
when he gave him his letter?
A: "Smell-a-gram!"
Tabitha, age 8
Massachusetts

Q: Why didn't the man believe the tiger?
A: He thought it was a lion!
Nicholas, age 9
New York

Q: What did the porcupine say when he ate a red pepper?

A: "This tastes very spiky!"

> Justin
> Canada

Q: Why did the bird rob the bank?

A: Because he was a robin!

> P.J., age 10
> Florida

Q: What kind of a monkey lives in the sky?

A: A moon-key!

> Faith, age 6
> Canada

Q: What has wings and solves number problems?

A: A moth-ematician!

> Crystal, age 11
> Tennessee

Q: What's the most faithful bug?

A: A tick, because they always stick to their friends!

> Amber, age 10
> Indiana

Q: Why did the kitten want to stay in the clinic?

A: Because it wanted to be a first-aid kit!

Anonymous

Q: What reptiles know how to use the telephone?

A: Croco-dials!

Justin

Q: What happens when a dog stays in the sun too long?

A: It turns into a hot dog!

Sandy, age 10
Louisiana

Q: What food do dogs dislike the most?

A: A hot dog!

Kiana, age 10
New York

Q: Did the shark have a good vacation?

A: Yes, it was en-jaw-able!

Tiffany, age 8
Arkansas

Q: Why don't the zoo keepers have to
   weigh the fish in the zoo's aquarium?
A: Because the fish have their own scales!
                    Callan
                    Canada

Q: Why did the snail want an "S" on his car?
A: So people would say, "Look at that
   'S'-car-go!"
                    Danny, age 10
                    Florida

Q: What is a zebra?
A: A horse with venetian blinds!
                    David, age 10
                    Illinois

Q: What does a spider do in a computer?
A: He makes a **World Wide Web**!
                    Jeremy, age 11
                    Missouri

Q: What's the difference between a
   tuna fish and a piano?
A: You can't tune a fish!
                    Stephanie, age 12
                    Florida

Q: What animal is likely to eat a relative?
A: An ant-eater!

Joel, age 11
Indiana

Q: Why did the cow eat a chocolate bar?
A: Because she wanted to have chocolate milk!
Lisa

Q: Why was the duck unhappy?
A: His bill was in the mail!

Michael, age 8
North Carolina

Q: What did the elephant say to the mouse?
A: "Pick on somebody your own size!"

Jessica, age 11
Tennessee

Q: Where do pigs keep their savings?
A: Piggy banks!

Nicci, age 12
Ohio

Q: What do you get if you pour boiling water down a rabbit hole?

A: Hot cross bunnies!

Esther, age 7
England

Q: What game do bunnies like best?

A: Hopscotch!

Caroline, age 12
North Carolina

Q: What do you get when you cross an elephant and a skunk?

A: A big stink!

Joey, age 9
Nebraska

Knock, knock.
Who's there?
Diesel.
Diesel, who?
Diesel all make you laugh!

> Nate, age 10
> Ohio

Knock, knock.
Who's there?
Yamaha.
Yamaha, who?
Yamaha wants you to go home!

> Bobby, age 11
> Pennsylvania

Knock, knock.
Who's there?
N.E.
N.E., who?
N.E. body can see I love Jesus!

> Eric, age 11
> Indiana

Knock, knock.
Who's there?
House.
House, who?
House it going?!

> Tiffany
> California

Knock, knock.
Who's there?
Olive.
Olive, who?
Olive forever in heaven!

> Kelsey, age 9
> Iowa

Knock, Knock
Who's there?
Frank.
Frank, who?
Frank you very much for opening the door!

> Magen, age 8
> Texas

Knock, knock.
Who's there?
Hutch.
Hutch, who?
Bless you!

> T.J., age 11
> Canada

Knock, knock.
Who's there?
Noah.
Noah, who?
Noah good knock-knock joke?!

> Melanie, age 11
> Canada

Knock, knock.
Who's there?
John.
John, who?
John the Baptist and I'm going to pour
    a bucket of water on you!

Jennifer, age 11
California

Knock, knock.
Who's there?
Howie.
Howie, who?
Fine, thanks. Howie you?!

Jordan, age 11
California

Knock, knock.
Who's there?
Dishes.
Dishes, who?
Dishes the police! Open up!

Elicia, age 9
New Hampshire

Knock, knock.
Who's there?
Banana.
Banana, who?
Knock, knock.
Who's there?
Banana.
Banana, who?
Knock, knock.
Who's there?
Orange.
Orange, who?
Orange you glad I didn't say banana?!

Felicia, age 10
Michigan

Knock, knock.
Who's there?
Boo.
Boo, who?
It's **OK**, don't cry!

Kristle, age 7
Canada

Knock, knock.
Who's there?
Little, old lady.
Little, old lady, who?
I didn't know you could yodel!

Chelsea, age 11
Minnesota

Knock, knock.
Who's there?
Shelby.
Shelby, who?
Shelby comin' round the mountain when she comes...!

Mary Anne, age 10
Tennessee

Knock, knock.
Who's there?
Ken.
Ken, who?
Ken you read me a story?!

Kimberly

Knock, knock.
Who's there?
Luke.
Luke, who?
Luke me up in the Bible!

Mikey, age 7
Michigan

Knock, knock.
Who's there?
10 Q.
10 Q, who?
10 Q very much!

Rebbica Ann, age 10

Knock, knock.
Who's there?
Wouldcha.
Wouldcha, who?
Wouldcha stop asking me questions and
    let me in?!

Heather, age 12

Knock, knock.
Who's there?
Dwayne.
Dwayne, who?
Dwayne the bathtub, I'm shriveling!

> Mistie, age 9
> Texas

Knock, knock.
Who's there?
Justin.
Justin, who?
Justin time for dinner!

> Gloryanna, age 9
> Kansas

Knock, knock.
Who's there?
I don't know, open the door and find out!

> Robert, age 8
> Canada

Knock, knock.
Who's there?
Lettuce.
Lettuce, who?
Lettuce in, it's cold out here!

> Haley, age 9
> Texas

Knock-Knock Jokes 59

Knock, knock.
Who's there?
Anita.
Anita, who?
Anita drink of water!
Josalyn, age 8
Texas

Knock, knock.
Who's there?
Gorilla.
Gorilla, who?
Gorilla hamburger, please!
Stuart, age 12
Jamaica

Knock, knock.
Who's there?
Odessa.
Odessa, who?
Odessa good thing to do!
Bobby, age 11
Pennsylvania

Knock, knock.
Who's there?
Amos.
Amos, who?
Amos-quito just bit me!
Desmonia, age 13
Louisiana

Knock, knock.
Who's there?
Canoe.
Canoe, who?
Canoe come out and play?!
Michael, age 8, Maine

Knock, knock.
Who's there?
Ja.
Ja, who?
Ja know the Lord loves you?!
Ashley, age 10
Texas

Knock, knock.
Who's there?
My.
My, who?
My God is awesome!
Tabitha, age 8
Massachusetts

Knock, knock.
Who's there?
Barbie.
Barbie, who?
Barbie-que chicken!
Mindy, age 9
Wisconsin

Knock, knock.
Who's there?
Philip.
Philip, who?
Philip the gas tank, please!
Rachael
Oklahoma

Knock, knock.
Who's there?
Chris.
Chris, who?
Christmas is coming!

Claudine, age 9
Texas

Knock, knock.
Who's there?
Praise.
Praise, who?
Praise the Lord, praise the Lord!

Donnell, age 12
North Carolina

Knock, knock.
Who's there?
Sherwood.
Sherwood, who?
Sherwood like to come in!

Amy, age 12
Kansas

Knock, knock.
Who's there?
Yoo.
Yoo, who?
Ooh! May I have some?!

Nicole
Georgia

Knock, knock.
Who's there?
Ali.
Ali, who?
Ali-bama!

Anonymous

Knock, knock.
Who's there?
Car.
Car, who?
Car if I come in?!

Lee, age 7
Texas

Knock, knock.
Who's there?
A.
A, who?
Amen!

Stacey, age 12
Missouri

Knock, knock.
Who's there?
Bless.
Bless, who?
Bless you!

Matthew, age 9
Georgia

Knock, knock.
Who's there?
Auto.
Auto, who?
Auto go to church every Sunday!

Nathan, age 11
Canada

Knock, knock.
Who's there?
Carrie.
Carrie, who?
Carrie these books, they're heavy!

Maggie, age 9
Missouri

Knock, knock.
Who's there?
Carmen.
Carmen, who?
Carmen get it!

Jared, age 13
California

Knock, knock.
Who's there?
Viper.
Viper, who?
Viper nose, it's running!

Monique, age 12
California

Knock, knock.
Who's there?
Water.
Water, who?
Water you waiting for? Open the door
   and let Jesus Christ in!

> Rebekkah, age 7
> North Carolina

Knock, knock.
Who's there?
Ham.
Ham, who?
Ham you got any hamburgers left?!

> Rebbica Ann, age 10

Knock, knock.
Who's there?
Alaska.
Alaska, who?
Alaska no questions, you tella no lies!

> Bobby, age 11
> Pennsylvania

Knock, knock.
Who's there?
Noah.
Noah, who?
Noah where the boat keys are?!

> Matthew, age 8
> North Carolina

Knock, knock.
Who's there?
Orange.
Orange, who?
Orange you gonna let me in?!
                    Misti
                    Texas

Q: What did the angel say when the
   kid said, "Hello"?
A: "Halo!"

Matt, age 9
California

Q: Who was the smallest man in history?
A: The sailor who slept on his watch!

Joel, age 11
Indiana

Q: Why is your nose in the middle of
   your face?
A: Because it's the scenter!

Jared, age 13
California

Q: What do you call a professor who
   travels far to give gifts?
A: A wise man!

Ken, age 14
Ohio

Q: Where did the sick ship go?
A: To see a dock!

Crystal, age 11
Tennessee

Q: When is a piece of wood like a king?
A: When it's made into a ruler!

> Yolanda, age 12
> Connecticut

Q: What did the baby light bulb say to the momma light bulb?
A: "I love you watts and watts!"

> Andrew, age 9
> Texas

Q: Why didn't the skeleton go to the dance?
A: Because it had no-body to go with!

> Dinah
> New Guinea

YUM!

Q: What is a computer's favorite junk food?
A: Micro-chips!

> Ato, age 12
> Connecticut

Q: Why did the golfer wear two pairs of pants?
A: Because he got a hole in one!
        Jill, age 7
        Alabama

Q: When does a sandwich ask a lot of questions?
A: When it's made of why bread!
        Latoya
        Alabama

Q: What do you call a prehistoric beach?
A: A dino-shore!
        Cody
        Kansas

Q: Why did the moon go to the bank?
A: To get his first quarter!
        Christopher, age 9
        Missouri

Q: What did Tennessee?
A: The same thing Arkansas!
        Anonymous

Q: What did the baby firecracker say
   to the other baby firecracker?
A: "My pop is bigger than your pop!"
                Sara, age 8
                Georgia

Q: When do people go to the beach?
A: On Sun-days!
                Nicholas, age 9
                New York

Q: What did the penny say to the other penny?
A: "Let's get together and make some cents!"
                Anonymous

Q: Why did the orange stop rolling
   down the hill?
A: Because it ran out of juice!
                Chetara, age 10
                Alabama

Q: What did the carrot say to the wheat?
A: "Lettuce rest, I'm feeling beet!"
                Bailey, age 9
                California

Q: What kind of shoes do you make out of banana skins?

A: Slippers!

> Rhema, age 7
> Texas

Q: What color is a shout?

A: Yell-oh!

> Rhiannon, age 9
> Texas

Q: What does a man eat to race?

A: A man-go!

> Kiana, age 10
> New York

Q: What did the flower say to the bee?

A: "Buzz off!"

> Leah, age 12
> Georgia

Q: Why did the girl run outside with her purse open?

A: She was expecting change in the weather!

> Stacy, age 13
> Arizona

Q: Where do you learn to make ice cream?
A: Sundae school!

Jessica, age 13
Florida

Q: Why did the boy throw his clock out the window?
A: He wanted to see time fly!

Latisha, age 9
North Carolina

Q: Why isn't your nose 12 inches long?
A: Because then it would be a foot!

Caleb
Canada

Q: What kind of sandwiches do astronauts eat?
A: Launch-meat sandwiches!

Melissa, age 10
South Carolina

Q: What do you call a telephone number
   that you dial with your foot?
A: A toe call!

> Matthew, age 12
> California

Q: What did the egg do when it heard
   a funny joke?
A: It cracked up!

> Rachel, age 11
> Pennsylvania

Q: What did the race announcer say when
   the mustard was behind the ketchup?
A: "Please pass the ketchup!"

> Lauren, age 11
> New York

Q: What did Mississippi sip?
A: A Mini-soda!

> Christina, age 8
> California

Q: What did one house say to the
   other house?
A: "House it going?!"

> Justin
> Canada

Q: What did the right shoe say to the left shoe after they ran through the mud?

A: "Is your soul clean?!"

Angelica, age 9
Ohio

Q: What did the customer say about the price of the fruit?

A: "The price is ripe!"

Sarah, age 7
Canada

Q: What did the mayonnaise say to the potato?

A: "Close the door, I'm dressing!"

Lee Anna, age 9
Canada

Q: Why did the man sleep under his car?

A: He wanted to get up oily in the morning!

Samantha, age 10
Australia

Q: What is it called when two trains tie in a race?

A: A railroad tie!

Rachel
Missouri

Q: Why is it sometimes windy on Wednesday?

A: Because it's winds-day!

Jenny
Florida

Q: What do you call a farmer who is in the spirit?

A: A jolly rancher!

Ken, age 14
Ohio

Q: How do you fix a broken pizza?

A: With tomato paste!

Rebecca, age 10
Canada

Q: What did the scarf say to the hat?

A: "I'll hang around and you go on a head!"

Dinah
New Guinea

Q: What did the policeman say to his tummy?
A: "You're under a vest!"
Sarah
England

Q: Why did the man read a joke to his mirror?
A: He wanted to crack it up!
Nicholas, age 9
New York

Q: What kind of sock always has holes in it?
A: A holy sock!
Marissa, age 8
Louisiana

Q: What did the momma bullet say to
the daddy bullet?
A: "We're going to have a BB!"
Jessica, age 11

Q: Why did the shoe go to the doctor?
A: Because he wanted to get heeled!
Lance, age 10
Arkansas

Q: What is the bar number on a cereal box called?
A: A cereal number!

Matt, age 9
California

Q: What did Delaware?
A: A New Jersey!

Hillary, age 10
Florida

Q: Where do you learn to greet people?
A: In "Hi" school!

Mal
New York

Q: Why did the lady put makeup on her head?
A: Because she wanted to make up her mind!

Christi, age 7
New York

Q: Why did the boy throw butter out the window?
A: He wanted to see a butterfly!

Jerson, age 10
Canada

Q: Why did the baby candle feel hot?
A: It had glowing pains!

> Lacey, age 8
> Washington

Q: What did the boy candle say to the girl candle?
A: "Want to go out with me tonight?"

> Norshanda, age 6
> Louisiana

Q: What do you get when you cross a light bulb and vegetables?
A: A light lunch!

> Nathaniel, age 11
> Texas

Q: What did George Washington say when he chopped down the cherry tree?
A: "It was an ax-ident!"

> Laura, age 6
> North Carolina

Q: What did one tonsil say to the other tonsil?
A: "The doctors are taking us out tonight!"

> Jessica, age 11
> Tennessee

Q: If a head of lettuce and a tomato
ran a race, which one would win?

A: The lettuce would be a-head,
but the tomato would ketchup!

Anonymous

Q: What is it like to have eight arms?

A: Very handy!

Brad, age 10
Arizona

Q: What state is named after a vegetable?

A: Okra-homa!

Allison, age 10
North Carolina

Q: Why was the arithmetic book so upset?

A: It was full of problems!

John, age 10
Australia

Q: What do you get when you cross a
pickle and a dollar bill?

A: Sourdough!

Jared, age 13
California

Q: Why did the egg go into the jungle?
A: He wanted to be an eggs-plorer!
Shari, age 11
New Jersey

Q: What do you call a smelly dinosaur egg?
A: Egg-stinked!
Ashley, age 11
Florida

Q: What do you call a banana that exercises?
A: A banana split!
Anna, age 9
Missouri

Q: What does a computer do at the beach?
A: Surf the net!

> Jeremy, age 11
> Missouri

Q: Which fruit is always grumpy?
A: A crab apple!

> Crystal, age 11
> Tennessee

Q: Why did the person put peanut butter
on the street?
A: To go with the traffic jam!

> Nicholas, age 9
> New York

Q: Why are soldiers always tired on the first of April?

A: Because they've just had a March of 31 days!

Joel, age 11
Indiana

Q: Why couldn't the audience hear the girl when she was singing by herself?

A: Because she sang so-low!

Anonymous

Q: What kind of flower grows between your nose and chin?

A: Tulips!

Melissa, age 12
Oklahoma

Q: Why did the little girl put candy
under her pillow at night?
A: Because she wanted to have sweet dreams!
Rachel, age 11
Pennsylvania

Q: What did the banana say to the orange?
A: "Orange you going to give me a shake?!"
Nathan, age 9
Colorado

Q: How do you make a hot dog stand?
A: Take away its chair!
Bethany, age 9

Q: What did one eye say to the other?
A: "Something smells between us!"
Theron, age 10
Texas

Q: What did the rug say to the floor?
A: "I've got you covered!"
Kristine, age 10
Canada

Q: Where does a snowman keep his money?
A: In a snowbank!

Matthew, age 12
Minnesota

Q: What is the richest kind of air?
A: A billionaire!

Courtney
South Carolina

Q: Why do people laugh at jokes about mountains?
A: Because they are hill-arious!

Brad, age 10
Arizona

Q: How do computers eat?
A: In mega-bytes!

Patrick, age 10
California

Q: What did one eye say to the other?
A: "It seems we have a common vision!"

Allison, age 10
Ohio

Q: What does a tree say when it wants
   to be by itself?
A: "Leaf me alone!"

Keeley
Texas

Q: Why did the teacher wear sunglasses?
A: Because her pupils were too bright!

Anna
Ireland

Q: What kind of train carries gum?
A: A chew-chew train!
Dominic, age 9
Texas

Q: Where would an alien put his teacup?
A: On a flying saucer!
Matt, age 9
Georgia

Q: What did one pie say to the other pie?
A: "I think I've got a crust on you!"
Anonymous

Q: Why was the rock star a mean musician?
A: He beat the drum and picked on the guitar!
Nicholas, age 9
New York

Q: What did the eye say to the other eye?
A: "Eye, eye!"
Katrina, age 11
England

Punny Jokes **87**

Q: What color is a cheerleader?
A: Yeller!

Anna, age 12
Georgia

Q: Why did the coach go to the bank?
A: To get his quarter-back!

Kenny, age 10
Oklahoma

Q: How did the farmer get the seeds to stay in the ground?
A: He sewed them in!

David
Arkansas

Q: What did the mustard say to the ketchup?
A: "You'd better ketchup!"

Barbie, age 12
Missouri

Q: How did the music teacher get locked out of his classroom?
A: His keys were inside the piano!

Justin

Q: What did the little boy feed his computer?
A: Chips!

Angela
Ohio

Q: What did the mud puddle say to the rain?
A: "Why don't you drop in some day?"
Chris
Virginia

Q: What did the nose say to the ear?
A: "Gotta run!"

Monique, age 12
California

Q: What do you call a doctor who melts
   in the sun?
A: A plastic surgeon!

Rhiannon, age 9
Texas

Q: What time do you go to the dentist?
A: 2:30 (tooth hurty)!

Gabriel, age 9
Arizona

Q: Why did the boy take a ladder to school?
A: He wanted to go to high school!
    Kenny, age 10
    Oklahoma

"Jokes That Aren't Bible Jokes or Animal Jokes or Knock-Knock Jokes or Punny Jokes, but They Are Jokes" Jokes

Q: If I had 40 apples in one hand and 50 in the
other, what would I have?
A: Big hands!

Chrissy, age 9

Q: What is worse than biting into an
apple with a worm in it?
A: Biting into an apple with half a worm in it!

Quenten, age 6
Texas

Q: Why did the radiator wear sunglasses?
A: To keep cool!

Ben

Q: What did the handstand man say to
the lady?
A: "You're upside down!"

Chrissy, age 9

Q: Why was the baby television crying?
A: Because it needed a channel change!

Lisa, age 12
Canada

Q: What is the difference between a teacher and a train?

A: Your teacher says, "Spit out your gum," but a train says, "Choo! Choo!"

Adrian, age 10
Oklahoma

Q: Why did the students throw eggs at the new drama teacher?

A: Because eggs go so well with ham!

Matthew, age 11
California

Q: Why is the Statue of Liberty hollow?

A: You'd be hollow, too, if you gave birth to a nation!

Katille, age 13
Missouri

Q: What did the ear say to the other ear?

A: "Between you and me, we have a brain!"

Katrina, age 11
England

Jokes That... **93**

Q: What did Paul Revere say after his ride?
A: "Whoa!"

Elijah
California

Q: If you're in a house with no doors
and windows and you're holding a
bat, how do you get out?
A: One, two, three strikes, you're out!

Joshua
West Virginia

Q: What is the easiest way to get on TV?
A: Sit on your set!

Travis, age 9
Oklahoma

Q: How many feet are in a yard?
A: It depends on how many people are
in the yard!

Laura, age 6
North Carolina

Q: Why do traffic lights never go swimming?
A: They spend too much time changing!
Shari, age 11
New Jersey

Q: Why are baseballs always mad?
A: Because the bats keep hitting them!
Erica, age 10
Texas

Q: What do you get when you cross
Cole with the law?
A: Coleslaw!
Isaac, age 12
Utah

Q: What kind of pet is found in cars?
A: A carpet!
Stephanie, age 12
Florida

Q: What do small people travel in?
A: A minivan!
Joy, age 9
Alabama

Q: What time is it when the clock strikes 13?
A: Time to fix the clock!

Danette, age 11
Arkansas

Q: Why did the boy go from home to the baseball field?
A: Because he wanted to go from home to home base!

Alicia, age 9
Mississippi

Q: What did the onion say to the small girl?
A: "If you cut me, I will make you cry!"

Ima, age 8
New Guinea

Q: What happens when one statue talks
  to another?
A: They say nothing!
                    Chrissy, age 9
                    West Virginia

Q: Why is a hill unlike a pill?
A: A hill is hard to get up and a pill is
  hard to get down!
                    Dorie
                    Georgia

Q: What do you get when you dial
   1-853-1013-76298-0056834?
A: A sore finger!

> Lance, age 10
> Arkansas

Q: What did one wall say to the other?
A: "Meet you at the corner!"

> Jenny, age 10
> Canada

Q: What is white, blue, red, white and blue?
A: Betsy Ross making the flag without
   her glasses!

> Chris, age 10
> Mississippi

Q: How much birdseed should you get for
   a quarter?
A: None. Quarters don't eat birdseed!

> Brad, age 10
> Arizona

Q: What did the minute hand say to the
   hour hand?
A: "I'll be around in an hour!"

> Melissa, age 12
> Oklahoma

Q: What did the ocean say to the shore?
A: Nothing, it just waved!
Anonymous

Q: What is the queen's favorite color?
A: Royal purple!

Tonya
Indiana

Q: Why do you go to bed at night?
A: Because the bed doesn't come to you!
Lauren, age 11
New York

Q: What do you do when you can't find
   any rubber bands?
A: Find a rubber orchestra!
                Anonymous

Q: Why did Benjamin Franklin invent electricity?
A: Because he wanted to play the electric guitar!
                Bryant, age 9
                Mississippi

Q: What do you call a saw with a hand?
A: A handsaw!
                Isaac, age 12
                Utah

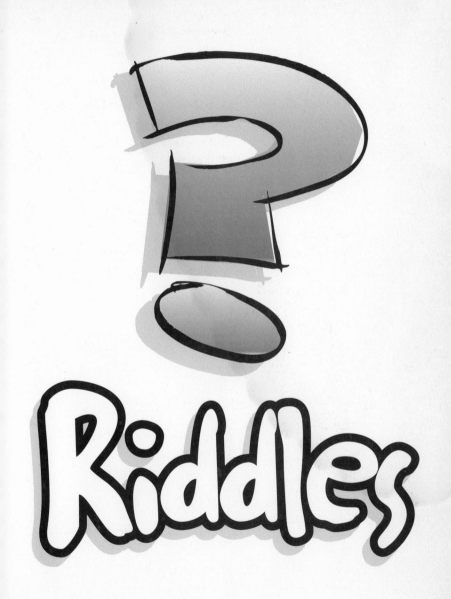

Riddles

Q: What word is always pronounced wrong?
A: Wrong!

> Laura
> Australia

Q: What is it that you can't hold for
10 minutes but is as light as a feather?
A: Your breath!

> Joel, age 11
> Indiana

Q: When can my grandpa step on blades
with bare feet and not cut himself?
A: When they're blades of grass!

> Nick, age 10
> Alabama

Q: What has one eye but can't see?
A: A needle!

> Tyeva, age 12
> North Carolina

Q: What has four legs but can't walk?
A: A chair!

> Korenza, age 13
> Canada

Q: Why didn't the skeleton play basketball?
A: He didn't have the guts!

Maggie, age 9
Missouri

Q: What has shoulders and a neck but no arms, legs or head?
A: A T-shirt!

Tiffany, age 10
Tennessee

Q: What do you get when you cross a telephone and an onion?
A: Onion rings!

Kristine, age 10
Canada

Q: What 10-letter word starts with G-A-S?
A: Automobile!

Kere, age 9
Pennsylvania

Q: What kind of buck can't be spent?
A: A male deer!

Elizabeth
New Jersey

Q: If a red house is on your right and a blue house
   is on your left, where is the white house?
A: In Washington, D.C.!

Cassandra, age 12
Ohio

Q: What two things can you never eat
   for breakfast?
A: Lunch and supper!

Dorie, age 12
Georgia

Q: What does a dog do that a man puts on?
A: Pants!

Jennie, age 9
Canada

Q: What tree barks the loudest?
A: A dogwood!

> Sandy, age 10
> Louisiana

Q: What never uses its teeth for eating?
A: A comb!

> Richado
> Texas

Q: If April showers bring May flowers,
    then what do May flowers bring?
A: Pilgrims!

> Dustin, age 9
> Arkansas

Q: What can run across the floor but
    has no arms or legs?
A: Water!

> Rebecca

Q: What kind of bow can't be tied?
A: A rainbow!

> Adrian, age 9
> Oregon

Q: What is able to knit without a
   needle and some thread?
A: A spider!

           Anonymous

Q: What has no feet but wears out shoes?
A: A sidewalk!

           Jessica, age 13
           Florida

Q: What is full of holes but can still
   hold water?
A: A sponge!

                Lynn, age 12
                Arkansas

Q: What has five eyes?
A: The M(i)ss(i)ss(i)pp(i) R(i)ver!
                Melissa, age 12
                Oklahoma

Q: What goes up and down but never sideways?
A: An elevator!

George
Virginia

Q: What touches people but can't feel?
A: Kind words!

Brent, age 11
Louisiana

Q: What has eyes, a tongue and a sole?
A: A shoe!

Brittany, age 10
Wisconsin

Q: What's black, white and read all over?
A: A newspaper!

Tyeva, age 12
North Carolina

Q: When will a net hold water?
A: When the water turns to ice!

Naurelle

Q: When can five people fit under one little umbrella and not get wet?
A: When it's not raining!
Naurelle

Q: What is no higher than the ground, yet you can't jump over it?
A: Your shadow!
Laura
Australia

Q: If a red house is made of red bricks and a blue house is made of blue bricks, what is a greenhouse made of?
A: Glass!
Becky, age 8
England

Q: What kind of dress is never worn?
A: An address!
Brittani, age 7
Louisiana

Q: When is a car not a car?
A: When it turns into a driveway!

Corrie, age 8
Canada

Q: When does Christmas come before Thanksgiving?
A: In the dictionary!

Joey, age 9
Nebraska

Q: Railroad crossing, look out for cars, how do you spell that without any "R's"?
A: T-H-A-T!

Dustin, age 9
Arkansas

Q: What has 34 feet, is yellow and carries books?
A: A school bus!

Monique, age 12
California

Q: What needs to be fixed every day but never breaks?
A: A bed!

Nick, age 10
Alabama

Riddles 109

Q: What has holes but is very strong?
A: A chain!

Anonymous

Q: What can you serve but not eat?
A: A tennis ball!

Stephanie, age 12
Florida

Q: What is the longest word in the English language?
A: Smiles, because there's a mile between the first letter and the last one.

Joel, age 11
Indiana

Q: What stands in the middle of Paris?
A: The letter "R"!

Samantha, age 12
England

Q: An electric train was going east at
   25 mph. The wind was going west
   at 35 mph. Which way was the
   smoke blowing?
A: Electric trains don't blow smoke!
                    Jerome, age 8
                    Minnesota

Q: What has four legs and ticks?
A: A dog!

                    Christine, age 9
                    Arizona

TICK TICK

Q: To what man does everyone take off
   his hat?
A: The barber!

> Joseph, age 11
> Oklahoma

Q: What runs around a yard without ever moving?
A: A fence!

> Mandy
> Canada

Q: What is round and orange with black stripes?
A: A basketball!

> Katie, age 9
> Kentucky

Q: One day a dime and a nickel were on a shelf.
   The nickel fell off. Why didn't the dime?
A: Because the dime had more cents!

> Sarah, age 11
> North Carolina

Q: What goes all over the country but
   never moves?
A: The road!

> Jeremy, age 10
> California

Q: What gets harder to catch the faster you run?
A: Your breath!

Christine, age 9
Arizona

Q: What can go up the chimney down but can't go down the chimney up?
A: An umbrella!

Danette, age 10
Arkansas

Q: How does a cowboy arrive on Friday, leave for three days and come back on Friday?
A: The horse's name is Friday!

Corey, age 14
Ohio

Q: What happens once in a minute, twice in a moment but never in a thousand years?
A: The letter "M"!

Jamie, age 11
Canada

Q: Which one is faster, hot or cold?
A: Hot, because you can catch a cold!
Dustin, age 9
Arkansas

Q: Why is the policeman the strongest
   man in town?
A: He can hold up many cars with one hand!
Dorie
Georgia

Funny Stories

A man dug his way out of jail into a
   preschool yard.
He said, "I'm free! I'm free!"
Then a little girl walked up to him and
   said, "So what? I'm four!"
                    Daniel, age 11
                    California

A.J.: Would you believe I was on the
   TV yesterday?
Jack: Wow!
A.J.: Yeah, but it was just for a minute.
   Then my mom said, "Get down!"
                    Nathan, age 8
                    North Carolina

Tim: It must be early morning.
Jim: How do you know?
Tim: It just dawned on me!
                    Jarrod, age 10
                    Texas

Catherine: It gets really cold on our
    Wisconsin dairy farm.
Dave: How cold does it get?
Catherine: It gets so cold our cows give
    ice cream!

> Catherine, age 4
> Wisconsin

Mom: Doctor, my child swallowed a pen.
    What should I do?
Doctor: Use a pencil!

> Jordan, age 10
> California

Little Miss Muffet sat on her tuffet,
    eating an ice cream cone.
Along came a spider and sat down beside her.
She said, "Go get your own!"

> Christine, age 9
> Arizona

Nit: Look over there and you'll see a
    20-foot snake!
Wit: Don't kid me. Snakes don't have feet!

> Seth
> Illinois

Roger walked into the pet shop and
    asked the clerk,
"How much does it cost for a goldfish?"
"They're a dollar a piece," she said.
"I see," said Roger, "and how much do
    you charge for a whole one?"
                    Sandy, age 10
                    Louisiana

Jessica: Will you remember me tomorrow?
Jenna: Yes.
Jessica: Will you remember me in two weeks?
Jenna: Yes.
Jessica: Will you remember me in a month?
Jenna: Yes.
Jessica: Knock, knock.
Jenna: Who's there?
Jessica: I thought you said you would
    remember me!
                    Jessica, age 7

Game Warden: Didn't you see the sign?
    It says, "No Fishing."
Boy: I'm not fishing. I'm teaching
    these worms how to swim!
                    David, age 10
                    Illinois

Diner: Tell me, waiter, do you have pig's feet?
Waiter: No, I'm just wearing funny-looking shoes!
                    Jarrod, age 10, Texas

Ted: What kind of bird is that?
Fred: It's a gulp.
Ted: I've never heard of a gulp.
Fred: It's like a swallow—but bigger!
Wesley, age 12

Daughter: What's the difference
between an elephant baby and a
matter baby?
Daddy: What's a matter baby?
Daughter: Nothing, I'm fine!
Alexis
Oregon

Diner: Waiter, what's this fly doing in
my soup?
Waiter: Looks like the backstroke, sir!
Sarah
Texas

Mary: We've got a new baby at our house.
Terry: Is he going to stay?
Mary: I guess so, he brought all his clothes!
Adria, age 5

Danielle: Can you stand on your head?
Mashelle: No, it's too high!
Jarrod, age 10
Texas

A tourist at the sea of Galilee wanted
to go sightseeing and found an idle
boatman who promised to show him
all the important points.
"Even where Jesus walked on the
water?" the tourist asked.
"Of course."
"How much?"
"Two hundred dollars."
The tourist replied, "Now I know why
He walked!"
Kenyatta, age 13
Florida

Mother: Doctor, my son thinks he's a chicken!
Doctor: Why didn't you bring him to me?
Mother: I wanted to, but we need the eggs!
                    Jessica, age 9
                    South Carolina

Kayla: Why do elephants paint their
       toenails red?
Chelsea: I don't know.
Kayla: To hide in cherry trees.
       Have you ever seen one in
       a cherry tree?
Chelsea: Oh, no.
Kayla: Works pretty well, huh?!
                    Chelsea, age 10
                    Minnesota

Hotel guest: Young man, please call me a taxi.
Doorman: Yessir. You're a taxi!
Rainey & Leadrew,
ages 3 & 4
Louisiana

J.K.: Is your refrigerator running?
S.K.: Yes.
J.K.: Well, you'd better go catch it!
Jacqueline, age 12
North Carolina

Doc: What happened to your ear?
Girl: The phone rang and I accidentally
picked up the hot iron.
Doc: What happened to your other ear?
Girl: They called back!
David

Prayer for Salvation

Father God, I believe that Jesus is Your Son and that You raised Him from the dead for me. Jesus, I give my life to You. Right now, I make You the Lord of my life and choose to follow You forever. I love You and I know You love me. Thank You, Jesus, for giving me a new life. Thank You for coming into my heart and being my Savior. I am a child of God! Amen.

Other Books Available

Baby Praise Board Book

Christmas Baby Praise Board Book

Noah's Ark Coloring Book

The Shout! Super-Activity Book

Commander Kellie and the Superkids_sm Books:

The SWORD Adventure Book

Commander Kellie and the Superkids_sm Series
Middle Grade Novels by Christopher P.N. Maselli

#1 The Mysterious Presence

#2 The Quest for the Second Half

#3 Escape From Jungle Island

#4 In Pursuit of the Enemy

World Offices of Kenneth Copeland Ministries

For more information about KCM and a free catalog, please write the office nearest you:

Kenneth Copeland Ministries
Fort Worth, Texas 76192-0001

Kenneth Copeland
Locked Bag 2600
Mansfield Delivery Centre
QUEENSLAND 4122
AUSTRALIA

Kenneth Copeland
Post Office Box 15
BATH
BA1 1GD
ENGLAND U.K.

Kenneth Copeland
Private Bag X 909
FONTAINEBLEAU
2032
REPUBLIC OF SOUTH AFRICA

Kenneth Copeland
Post Office Box 378
Surrey
BRITISH COLUMBIA
V3T 5B6
CANADA

UKRAINE
L'VIV 290000
Post Office Box 84
Kenneth Copeland Ministries
L'VIV 290000
UKRAINE

We're Here for You!

Believer's Voice of Victory Magazine

Enjoy inspired teaching and encouragement from Kenneth and Gloria Copeland each month in the *Believer's Voice of Victory* magazine. Also included are real-life testimonies of God's miraculous power and divine intervention into the lives of people just like you!

It's more than just a magazine—it's a ministry.

Believer's Voice of Victory Television Broadcast

Join Kenneth and Gloria Copeland, and the *Believer's Voice of Victory* broadcasts, Monday through Friday and on Sunday each week, and learn how faith in God's Word can take your life from ordinary to extraordinary. This is some of the best teaching you'll ever hear, designed to get you where you want to be—*on top!*

You can catch the *Believer's Voice of Victory* broadcast on your local, cable or satellite channels.

*Check your local listings for times and stations in your area.

Shout!...The dynamic magazine just for kids!

Shout! The Voice of Victory for Kids is a Bible-charged, action-packed, bimonthly magazine available FREE to kids everywhere! Featuring *Wichita Slim* and *Commander Kellie and the Superkids, Shout!* is filled with colorful adventure comics, challenging games and puzzles, exciting short stories, solve-it-yourself mysteries and much more!!

Stand up, sign up and get ready to Shout!

To receive a FREE subscription to *Believer's Voice of Victory,* or to give a child you know a FREE subscription to *Shout!,* write:

Kenneth Copeland Ministries
Fort Worth, Texas 76192-0001

Or call: 1-800-600-7395 (9 a.m.-5 p.m. CT)
Or visit our website at: www.kcm.org

If you are writing from outside the U.S., please contact the KCM office nearest you. Addresses for all Kenneth Copeland Ministries offices are listed on the previous page.